WHAT KIND OF A FATHER WAS HE?

Polly sometimes felt as if she didn't know her own father! How could he keep returning to the Indians, their enemies, bringing them medicine? Didn't he remember what they had done, every time he looked up at Massacre Hill? Her father, "Doc Sutter," as everybody called him, was getting to be an Indian-lover.

Polly desperately wanted to run away from the frontier, the Indians, and the father she couldn't understand. Especially after Father returned with the seriously sick girl who now occupied Polly's own bed. An Indian. How could he do this to her—expect his own daughter to give up her room, her dreams, her very way of life?

What kind of a Christmas present was this?

A TOMAHAWK FOR CHRISTMAS

Another Chappie Creek Adventure

Mary La Pietra

Illustrated by
Arnold Kohn

David C. Cook Publishing Co.

ELGIN, ILLINOIS—WESTON, ONTARIO
LA HABRA, CALIFORNIA

David C. Cook Publishing Co., Elgin, IL 60120

Printed in the United States of America
Library of Congress Catalog Number: 76-11478
ISBN: 0-89191-052-2

To all the Polly Sutters everywhere in the world . . .

. . . that they, too, may learn to "bury the hatchet."

Author's Note

Chappie Creek was never on any map, nor was there ever any tribe of American Indians called the Tomahawks.

But I hope this will not make *A Tomahawk for Christmas* any less believable—or enjoyable—for its readers.

CONTENTS

Someone Missing

1

Someone Missing

CHRISTMAS EVE, 1821, Polly Sutter wrote in her diary. *Our fifth Christmas without Mama. Our first without Papa. And all because of those worthless Tomahawks!*

She snapped the little book shut and turned angry blue eyes from the fireplace to the cabin window. She could never escape them—she was completely surrounded by *Indians*.

Outside the log cabin the brown and bent stalks of the summer's corn stuck up here and there through the snow like stubborn reminders. Thirteen-year-old Polly had heard it so many times: if it had not been for Indian corn, many of the early settlers would not have survived their first winters in this land.

How easily some people forgot. If they would look beyond those stalks of corn, up to Massacre

Hill where the crude grave markers also stuck up above the snow, they would remember something else they had to thank the Indians for. There were many settlers who never saw another winter—not because of cold or hunger—but because they had been killed one summer day when a band of Tomahawk braves had swooped down upon them from that very hill.

Even inside, in the warmth of the cabin, Polly could not escape the Indians. That same all-saving corn hung in clusters above the fireplace, drying. The rug before the hearth, woven by one of the Indian squaws, had been given to her father in exchange for doctoring the woman's baby back to health.

Indeed, the very shoes on her feet—buckskin moccasins—were something "borrowed" from the Indians. As was all the outer clothing worn by the settlers during the cold winter: jackets, leggings, and shoepacks made from the skins of animals that had been hunted down by the Indians. More often than not, skins were offered by the Tomahawks in exchange for the settlers' all-precious and much-desired maple sugar from the East.

For Polly, even worse than borrowing anything from the Indians was having to "lend" them something. In this case, it was her very own father.

14

She would never be able to understand it. How could her father turn his back on Massacre Hill and ride out in a blizzard to carry medicine and healing to the very savages that had killed so many of his friends and neighbors?

And Mama. How could he forget about *Mama?*

"Why did they have to get sick at *Christmastime?*" she said angrily from the fireside bench. She tossed her flaxen hair toward the Tomahawk camp.

"Nobody *picks* the time to get sick," said her twin brother, Paul, who sat cross-legged on the rug, cleaning his gun.

"Why don't they use their *own* medicine man?" She got up from the bench, took an iron, and peevishly began poking at one of the burning logs.

"He probably isn't feeling too well himself," said Paul with a sly grin. Both he and Polly knew that with the coming of the Great White Doctor and his powerful remedies, the medicine man of the Tomahawk tribe had become less and less important. His main role among the tribe now seemed to be that of performing weather chants and dances. This summer even that had been a waste of time, since all his frantic wailing and rattling had failed to bring rain when it was needed.

15

"I don't know why Papa bothers with them at all," said Polly, giving the log another fretful poke. "What have they ever done for us—except given us trouble?"

"I know what's bothering *you*," said Paul, rising and setting the rifle back into its rack above the fireplace. "It's having to change all those fancy plans you had for Christmas."

"Yes!" she said, standing erect. "And why *shouldn't* I be upset? This is the second time we planned a trip east and had to postpone it because of those worthless Indians!"

Maybe if Mama hadn't died—or if Paul had been a girl instead of a boy—maybe the trip east would not seem so terribly important. But, ever since Emilie Coulter's cousin had come from Boston to live in Chappie Creek, Polly had yearned to go east.

Of course, Polly never had anything to do with Mary Elizabeth Coulter, for the same reason she no longer was friends with Emilie: their grandmother was part Indian. But that had not kept her from listening that day at the schoolhouse when Mr. Whittington had asked Mary Elizabeth to tell the other students about life in Boston. Polly had recorded in her diary:

We heard of the many friends Mary Elizabeth had had, the fine clothes they all wore, the big school they attended, and the grand parties they were always going to.

16

Here, in the prairie settlement called Chappie Creek, the only parties were roof-raisings, sewing bees, or socials at the little two-by-four church in the valley.

And Christmas! What a grand and glorious time was Christmas in Boston! There were sleigh rides and caroling and mountains of gifts beneath the tree. The tree—as high as the ceiling—had dozens of burning candles and was wound all about with long chains of maple sugar candy.

Imagine having enough candles to burn on a tree! Or enough sugar to make candy!

Christmas in Chappie Creek usually meant a little more honey in the beans—or maybe just a few more beans. As for gifts, there might be a new pair of rawhide laces for your moccasins. This Christmas it would be even worse. This Christmas they wouldn't even have a tree and Papa wouldn't be at the table to say grace.

None of this seemed to trouble her brother Paul. In fact, he was disgustingly cheerful about the whole thing. And Polly knew why. All Paul was concerned about was whether or not Papa would bring back from the Indian camp what he had asked for: a tomahawk.

She knew why Paul wanted the tomahawk. Not for himself, but to exchange with Homer Farnsworth at the trading post for a newer, more powerful gun. With a better gun, said Paul, he would be a better hunter and that would mean more food on the Sutter table.

Maybe so. But, Polly also knew that with a more powerful gun Paul Sutter would command more respect among the other boys in the settlement.

What Trader Farnsworth wanted with some old worthless tomahawk was something Polly had not yet figured out.

Paul threw another log onto the fire. "If I were you, Polly, I'd forget about Boston—unless you want to make the trip alone."

"Alone!" she exclaimed. "Why should I have to go *alone?*"

"I don't think Pa would ever go that far and stay that long away from Chappie Creek."

Polly was stunned. "But, Papa said—"

"I know," Paul nodded, "that he'd take you to visit our cousins in Boston. Probably means it, but when it comes right down to going—I don't think he will. He'd worry himself to death about what's going on back here."

"You mean *there,*" she said bitterly, nodding in the direction of the Indian camp. Sometimes it seemed that her father spent more time tending the Tomahawks than the folks in Chappie Creek.

"Besides," said Paul, "we couldn't have gone

18

anyway. With all this snow, there won't be a stage in or out of here 'til spring."

Polly was suddenly annoyed with her brother. Ever since Paul had gotten his own gun, he had begun to talk and act as if he and Polly had been born years—instead of minutes—apart. As if simply having a gun in his hands gave him some sort of special wisdom. It irked Polly that he could so calmly dismiss the trip east that meant so much to her. And the way he wanted her to believe that he knew their father's innermost thoughts.

"You think you're so smart, that you know everything!"

"A good deal more than you."

With that, she snatched up her diary, stormed into the bedroom, and slammed the door.

Someone Coming

2

Someone Coming

POLLY PEEVISHLY THREW HERSELF down on her bed.

It was really quite an elegant bed for a log cabin in Chappie Creek: a canopied four-poster brought all the way by wagon from the East. Never a day went by that Polly didn't carefully dust the white canopy, rearranging the ruffles so they would hang just so. And the first warm spring day would find her washing it, dunking it into a bucket of corn starch, and hanging it out on the line to crisp in the breeze.

Next to her mother's cameo brooch, the canopy bed was Polly's most treasured possession. Papa had bought the bed for Mama and it had been delivered just a month before *it* had happened.

Lying under the canopy, Polly would try to remember Mama—how she had been before she had gotten sick. Sometimes it was hard to even remember her at all, how her face had looked or how her voice had sounded.

Lying beneath the starched ruffles, Polly would then let her thoughts stray eastward to all the many comforts there which surely must make life more bearable for a girl of 13. Like an untended toothache, her yearning to travel east to visit her cousins never left her.

I'd forget about Boston . . .

Was Paul right about Papa? Would her father never go back to Boston, even for just a visit? Boston—where he had been born, studied to be a doctor, met and married Polly's mother?

. . . unless you want to make the trip alone.

Why not? she thought. *Why not make the trip alone?* Hadn't Mary Elizabeth Coulter come all the way from Boston to Chappie Creek all by herself? Why couldn't Polly Sutter do just the opposite?

She suddenly sat up on the bed. That was it—that was exactly what she would do! She would find something valuable to trade with Homer Farnsworth for the fare, and in the spring when the snow was gone and the trail open again, she would simply get on the stagecoach and head east.

If she liked Boston as much as she was sure she would—who knew? She might *never* return to Chappie Creek!

"Soup—again?" said Paul from the bench.

Her secret plan cheered Polly as she came out of the bedroom and went to the fireplace to put on the kettle.

"Soup—again?" said Paul, from the bench where he now sat whittling with his jackknife on a small piece of wood.

"I was sure you wouldn't want *pheasant* again," said Polly. Actually, it was all of two months since any of them had had a taste of pheasant. In fact, the last fresh meat they had eaten was the rabbit Paul had shot out in the front yard two days ago.

"If you're so tired of bean soup, why don't you go out and *shoot* something?" *And cut us a Christmas tree,* she added in her mind.

"You know what Pa told me before he left," said Paul, making another notch with his knife. "I'm not to leave you alone."

"That's silly." But in truth, Polly was grateful for her father's order—even if it meant no Christmas tree and being cooped up all day with her brother.

Polly hadn't yet gotten over her fright of just three days ago when, trudging back to the cabin from the smokehouse, she had found a big Indian blocking her path. He had come to fetch the White Doctor. But at that moment there was no one who could have convinced Polly Sutter that his mission was anything else but to send her up to join the others on Massacre Hill.

She had run, screaming, to the cabin, and it had taken her father almost an hour to quiet her down. Surely, then, he must have remembered how it had been with Mama. Surely he wouldn't go packing off in a blizzard to tend one of those worthless Tomahawks!

"You want to know what I'm going to do if he brings it?" she suddenly spoke from the hearth.

"What?" said Paul. "And who?"

"Papa," said Polly, "if he brings back a tomahawk. First chance I get, I'm going to toss it into the creek!"

"Then I'll just have to make sure you don't *get* the chance," her brother said, still whittling. "Besides, the creek's frozen solid."

Polly slammed her wooden spoon down on the fireside bench. "How could you even *touch* it?" she cried. "For all you know, it could be the very thing that scalped some of *them!*" She pointed with the spoon toward Massacre Hill.

"That was a long time ago," said Paul. "Before we were even born."

"And Mama? What about *her?*"

Paul suddenly stopped whittling and sat up straight on the bench. "*Shush!* I think I heard something."

Polly opened her eyes wide. "What?"

"Someone coming." Quick as a rabbit, Paul was off the bench and had an ear to the door.

Polly tightened her grip on the wooden spoon

27

and listened. Hunting had no doubt sharpened her brother's ears. "I don't hear anything."

"Sounds like a sled."

A sled meant that the "someone coming" was *not* their father. Doc Sutter had left on horseback only, with his medicines in a saddlebag. It was probably one of those worthless Tomahawks coming into the settlement to sell skins. Or more likely to steal, she thought.

Paul went to the window and peered out through the frost. As the sound of slats on snow finally reached Polly's ears, her brother sprang from the window and tore open the cabin door.

"It's *Pa!*"

Polly didn't believe it until she had her arms around him. His nose red from the cold and his whiskers crisp with frost, it *was* her father!

"Oh, Papa!" she cried happily. "You're *home!*"

Doc Sutter gave his daughter a frosty kiss and then quickly freed himself. "Got to unload that sled. Paul, get your jacket!"

Paul went to the peg for his buckskin jacket and Polly, spoon in hand, returned to the hearth. She was glad she had already put the kettle on, for if anyone looked as if he needed a cup of hot, hearty bean soup it was her frostbitten and travel-weary father.

"Did you bring the tomahawk?" asked Paul, getting into his jacket.

"Surely did," said his father, opening the

Papa had a large, lumpy bundle in his arms.

door. "One for your sister, too."

The wooden spoon went clattering onto the stone hearth. Polly stood with her mouth open, staring at the door after Paul and her father went out. Surely Papa must be joking! He knew how she felt about those worthless Indians!

Why in the world would he bring her a tomahawk?

When he came back into the cabin, her father had a large, lumpy bundle in his arms. It was almost as big as Polly herself. From the bottom of the bundle peeked two slender brown feet. From the top dangled two long black braids.

"Pull down your quilt, Polly," said Doc Sutter. "We've a very sick girl here."

A Dying Flower

3

A Dying Flower

IT WAS MORE THAN POLLY COULD BEAR. Having an Indian under the same roof was bad enough. Letting her lie on Polly's precious canopy bed was just *too much*.

"I'll kill her," she whispered under her breath, but loud enough for her brother to hear.

"Looks to me she's half dead already," said Paul.

From the hearth, Polly glanced into the bedroom where the girl's dark head was like an ugly blot on her white pillow. The girl hadn't spoken or opened her eyes since Papa had laid her down on the bed. All she did was cough. A terrible, racking cough that shook the four-poster and sent the starched ruffles aflutter. Maybe she *would* die.

In the tongue of the Tomahawks her name was almost impossible to pronounce. Or perhaps that was because Polly Sutter did not wish to pronounce it. In English, it was Wilting Sunflower.

At birth, about 16 years ago, it had been Shining Sunflower—but an Indian name did not always remain the same. This was especially true in the case of the braves whose names were shaped by their own deeds or events of their lives. An Indian boy might greet the world with the name of Hungry Wolf and take to the grave the name of Growling Bear.

Shining Sunflower had become Wilting Sunflower when everyone could see that she was smaller and frailer than other girls.

All this Polly learned, reluctantly, from her father as he began preparing medicine for his young patient. He set another kettle on the hearth beside Polly's yet unserved soup. In her father's kettle simmered a mixture of honey, some sticky substance from a pine tree, and several drops of a special medicine that he ordered every now and then from the East.

The brew actually had a pleasant aroma— mostly of pine—and as it filled the cabin Polly was reminded that they had no Christmas tree. It seemed Papa wasn't even aware it was Christmas Eve. Or that there had even been any talk of traveling east.

His thoughts and plans of the moment were all centered on the sick Indian girl—and how Polly was to help him in tending her.

"Pneumonia," said Doc Sutter, "is like a visiting, but unwelcome relative. You have to cater to it, all the while hoping it'll someday get up and leave."

The only one Polly wanted to get up and leave was Wilting Sunflower. As for catering to her—she was determined not to lift so much as a finger to help this most unwelcome guest.

"Put the soup on the back hook, Polly," said her father. "And then get out the warming pan. Paul's bringing in some more logs."

Polly calmly kept stirring her bean soup. She knew the pan would be used for warming up the bed for Wilting Sunflower.

"Did you hear what I said, girl?"

"Yes, Papa. I heard what you said."

"Then why—"

Doc Sutter cut himself short and stood looking down at his daughter. Then he briefly nodded as if suddenly he understood.

"She's a human being, Polly. A person. She hurts just as much as you do—no matter the color of her skin."

It was like a slap in the face. Her father seemed to be telling her that all along her feelings about the Indians had been wrong.

How could it be wrong to hate people who

35

could swoop down on a settlement and kill so many men, women, and children?

How could it be wrong to hate those who had caused your own mother's death?

Doc Sutter's voice suddenly had a different sound to it, as if he might be some inquiring stranger she had met on the road. "Tell me, Polly, what is it you call yourself—a Christian?"

What kind of question was that? Didn't they go to the same church, read the same Bible and pray together each night? Hadn't he, himself, taught her how to pray?

"And as a Christian, what do you believe?" continued her father in that same cold and unfriendly voice. "That we are all God's children—all except the Indians? Then who created the Indians, Polly?"

Tears began to well up in Polly's eyes. She didn't know what hurt more—the coldness in her father's voice or the confusion he was causing in her mind.

"Papa—I thought you understood!"

"I *do* understand, Polly. You want to be a Christian—but only when it's easy."

"That's not so!"

"Then prove it! A true Christian is able to forgive."

"Papa—I *can't!*"

"Not even on *Christmas?*"

The tears blurred her vision as she swallowed hard and looked toward the bedroom and the quiet mound under her own quilt.

Her father's voice suddenly was his own again and his hand was gentle on her shoulder. "Polly, that girl may very well die tonight if we don't—*all* of us—help her."

Sad Memories

4

Sad Memories

CHRISTMAS CAME AND WENT without so much as an extra candle being lit. All Polly got in her stocking was a blister from so many trips between the hearth and the bedroom. Papa was constantly ordering her to bring more hot broth or to reheat the warming pan so he could keep moving Wilting Sunflower to a warmer side of the bed.

The only one who got to attend Christmas services was Paul, and Polly suspected her brother had gone only to catch another glimpse of Mary Elizabeth Coulter.

Paul was beginning to think (or at least talk) like some of the men in the settlement, as if he thought religion was for women and children.

"Sarah can do the praying and I'll do the draying" was the way Tom Piper put it. Tom's business in Chappie Creek was that of draying—or hauling—things for people from one part of town to another.

There were many other men whose work did not rhyme with "praying" but whose sentiments were the same. A man had too much to do (planting, harvesting, smithing, or milling) to spend time praying. Besides, the womenfolk liked getting all dressed up for Sunday services.

Polly's father did not share this kind of thinking. Never a meal went by that he did not lead his small family in saying grace, and if ever he missed a Sunday service it was only because he was out on some call as a doctor.

He was strict, too, about the Bible. It might be just a passage or two, but before the Sutter family closed their eyes at night there was always a reading. And then a family prayer.

Sometimes the doctor's prayer would include the name of one of his patients, asking God to guide him in treating some strange illness. Doc Sutter never claimed to have worked any miracles, but he did tell his family that there were some folks alive in Chappie Creek today only "by the grace of God."

His first night home, the doctor's prayer had, of course, included the name of Wilting Sunflower. And although Polly had added her "Amen"—in her heart she did not mean it.

And when she did her father's bidding,

brought another quilt or reheated the warming pan, it was not in any way an act of mercy. It was merely to keep peace.

When she finally lay down that night on her brother's cot, bone-tired, Polly didn't care the least that Wilting Sunflower was in her crisis, and if she did not pass it, she would die. Polly thought only of her father, sitting in the chair beside the canopy bed, and the fact that he would get no sleep that night.

And then her thoughts drifted back to another night—five years ago—and someone else who had not been able to sleep.

Only eight years old then, Polly had not known her mother was expecting another child. Later, she remembered that Mama had looked a bit rounder beneath her apron.

She would never forget the terrible, frightened screams when her mother went to the smokehouse early one morning and found the two Indians there, stealing bacon. Her mother didn't stop screaming until it was all over. And then she lay silently staring up at the white ruffled canopy as Papa carried the dead baby out to bury it near the lilac bush in the backyard.

And then that was the way it always was: Mama lying in bed for weeks and weeks, just staring up at the canopy and never saying another word.

43

When she did finally get out of bed it was in the dark of a snowy December night when everyone else was asleep. Homer Farnsworth found her the next morning, huddled against the door of the trading post in only her nightgown—stiff and cold. And dead.

A true Christian is able to forgive.

Then Polly was not a true Christian. For she would never be able to forgive those thieving Indians who had so badly frightened her mother and caused her to lose both her unborn baby and her very own mind.

In the morning when her father told her that Wilting Sunflower had passed the crisis, Polly thought: *Good. Now you can take her back to where she belongs–with her tribe. And you can give me back my mother's bed.*

"But she's going to need a heap of care and a good long rest," said Doc Sutter. "It may take 'til spring before our little Sunflower is shining again."

Mama's Brooch

5

Mama's Brooch

OUR LITTLE SUNFLOWER! Every time she heard it, Polly thought she was going to get sick—and that was at least four or five times a day.

"Well! Our Little Sunflower is quite perky today," her father might say in the morning.

Or in the afternoon: "Fine! I see our Little Sunflower is taking a nap."

He never once asked Polly how *she* might be feeling with the burden of another mouth to feed, dozens of doses of medicine to give, and the chore of continually moving Sunflower from one side to another. It was important in treating pneumonia, said Doc Sutter, to keep the patient moving.

He himself was again on the move—tending to the various winter ailments and complaints in Chappie Creek. With Paul out hunting every day with his new gun, the job of nursing Sunflower back to health was left mostly in Polly's hands.

And though her heart certainly was not in it, she seemed to be doing a good job. Each day the girl's dark face seemed a bit fuller and her eyes brighter. Yet Polly still found it hard to believe that the Indian girl was older than she—by almost three years.

She got angry with herself when she wondered *anything* about their unwelcome guest. The only thing Polly wanted to keep in her mind was the thought that the better she nursed Little Sunflower, the sooner she would be completely well and out of the canopy bed.

Although Polly had had to give up her beloved bed, she had not been asked to move any of her belongings out of the bedroom. So, along with her nursing, she would still fuss with the canopy ruffles, dust her bureau, and rearrange her few treasures that were spread out on the bureau beside the bottles of medicine: her mother-of-pearl comb, brush, and mirror; her diary, and her mother's precious cameo brooch.

One day as Polly was dusting, she could not find the brooch. Thinking it might have been knocked off the bureau, she looked all over the room for it: under the bureau, under the hooked rug, and even under the bed. When she lifted

"That girl is a thief!" Polly cried.

her head up from under the bed, she was face to face with Wilting Sunflower, who lay smiling and turning the little ornament over and over in her hands.

"That girl is a thief!" she cried, running from the bedroom. "She stole my cameo!"

"Don't be ridiculous," said Paul, from the fireplace. "She barely has the strength to feed herself. How could she get out of bed to steal *anything*?"

"She *has* the brooch," Polly insisted. "How else could she get it?"

Up to this time, their father had been sitting before the fire, studying the flames. Suddenly he turned to Polly. "It's simple," he said quietly. "I let her . . . "

Polly could not believe her ears. "You *let* her . . . my mother's brooch?" She burst into tears. "Papa, how *could* you?"

Doc Sutter tried to calm her. "I knew she was curious about it. I brought it to her so she could see it more closely. I didn't know she would misunderstand. She thought I was *giving* it to her. I'm sorry, Polly."

"Then *make* her understand!" sobbed Polly. "Take it *back* from her!"

"I'm sorry, Polly!" Her father was genuinely moved. "But we just can't do that."

"Of course not," laughed Paul. "We wouldn't want her to think we were *Indian* givers."

Angry and hurt, Polly stormed out of the cabin in her buckskin jacket and shoepacks. She didn't know where she would go, but trudging through the snow, she ended up at the Chappie Creek Trading Post. Even the noisy and smelly old post was better than a cabin where her own father could so calmly allow a worthless Indian girl to have one of her most treasured possessions.

At the post, Polly wandered through the kerosene lamps and kegs of horseshoes, eventually ending up in the corner where Trader Farnsworth kept the sewing thread, buttons, and bolts of fabrics. She never came to the post that she didn't fondle some of the finer fabrics and trimmings, knowing full well how impractical a lace-trimmed frock of sky blue satin with pearl buttons would be for a girl who lived in Chappie Creek.

But, for a girl who lived in the East . . .

A Creepy Encounter

6

A Creepy Encounter

"ANY NEWS OF THE STAGE?" she asked Trader Farnsworth over the counter.

"Not yet," said the old man. "Seems they had a lot more snow back east."

Polly sighed. And then her eye was caught by the dozen or so fancy, befeathered tomahawks that hung, along with buggy whips and harnesses, on the wall behind the counter. Why Homer Farnsworth collected those horrible things she could not understand.

Although the look of any tomahawk made her shudder, Polly could not help but admire some of them—especially the ones with the hand-carved handles. All of them had shiny and very sharp-looking blades. All except the one she recognized as the tomahawk her father had brought back for Paul, at Christmas.

"Tell me something, Mister Farnsworth," she said, nodding to the wall behind him. "What do you want with that old tomahawk when you have all those others?"

"You mean the one your brother brought in?"

Polly nodded. "Yes."

"Well, you see—I was looking for a *real* one."

Polly was somewhat bewildered. "What are *those*? Aren't those real?"

The old man shook his head. "Those fancy ones all come from the East. Some as far as the Old Country."

"The Old Country!" Now she really was confused.

"Yup," he nodded. "Somebody saw a chance to make some hay off the Indians—"

"You mean the Indians buy tomahawks made by *white men?*"

"That's right," he nodded again. "They're much better than the old stone ones they used to make with their bare hands."

Polly shook her head. This was almost as hard to accept as what Mr. Whittington had told his class one day: that it was the white man who was responsible for the spread of the terrible practice of scalping.

When the French and English had been battling for territory, said Mr. Whittington, the French had enlisted the aid of the Indians, promising a reward for every English scalp brought in. The British then offered a bounty for both French and Indian scalps—as though they were no more than the pelt of some bothersome animal.

"Then what would you want the *old* tomahawk for?" she again asked Trader Farnsworth.

"Oh, *I* don't want it," he said. "It's for Otis Grimes. And don't ask me what *he* wants it for—nobody can figure out what's going on in *his* head." He tapped his own forehead the way most folks did when they talked about Otis Grimes. It was their way of saying that Otis Grimes was "tetched"—or out of his head.

To Polly, Otis Grimes seemed almost like a legend. Though people often talked about him, he rarely came into town—spending most of his time alone in the broken-down cabin that was his home. Folks said Otis Grimes once had the biggest and most prosperous farm in the valley. Now the fields lay overgrown with weeds, and each year the cabin seemed to sink a little bit lower into the ground. Sort of like Otis himself.

Polly's father said Otis Grimes' sickness was not in his head, but rather in his heart. It was the most hopeless sickness a man could have. Although he never came right out and said it, Polly knew her father meant that Otis Grimes' "sickness" was his hatred for the Tomahawk

Indians who had killed his wife and baby daughter that terrible day—almost 15 years ago.

And that was easy to understand—especially for Polly. Yet that made his want of a tomahawk all the more puzzling. Unless it was that after all these years Otis Grimes was going to "bury the hatchet."

Burying the hatchet—or tomahawk—was the custom when peace had been made between warring tribes or between the white man and the Indian. Perhaps that was what Otis Grimes planned to do with the old tomahawk: *bury* it, along with his 15-year-old hatred.

But Polly couldn't imagine anyone being able to forgive someone who had killed his wife and baby.

There had been other times when Polly had been thinking or talking about a certain person and then, who should pop right up on the scene but that very person! Only this time, it gave her the creeps.

Because she had not seen Otis Grimes for almost a year, when she turned around and saw him coming in through the trading post door, she gave out a little gasp. Mostly because he looked so terrible, with his beard all crusty and matted together and his eyes—peering out from deep, dark sockets—darting here and there.

He swiped at his nose with a grimy sleeve and

then stood in the doorway, blocking Polly's path as she tried to leave.

"Doc Sutter's girl, ain't yuh?" he asked, again swiping at his nose.

"Yes." She moved again toward the door, but he didn't budge.

His eyes reminded her of some wild animal. "True what I hear? About you folks having an Injun up to yer cabin?"

"Yes," Polly said. *And my own father gave her my mother's brooch.* "Only because she's sick."

"Gonna *die?*" he asked, those animal eyes fastened on hers.

"Not if my father can help it," she said bitterly.

Otis Grimes swiped a third time at his nose and looked off in the direction of Polly's home.

"Maybe," he said slowly, "maybe your pa won't be *able* to help it."

If she had hoped a trudge in the cold would cool her anger, it had done just the opposite. Seeing Otis Grimes—what 15 years of grief had done to him—only stirred up the coals of her own hatred for the Indians. And regardless of what her father had said, Polly was determined, now, to take back her mother's brooch. If the girl made any struggle, Polly would force it from her.

But when she got to the cabin, the brooch was

59

back in its place on her bureau and Wilting Sunflower had her face turned to the wall.

Both Polly's father and brother denied having taken the brooch from the girl.

It was the first sign that Wilting Sunflower was able to get out of bed. And the first hint Polly had had that the Indian girl was able to understand English.

Fireside Lessons

7

Fireside Lessons

WHAT COULD BE WORSE than having a sick Indian girl in your very own bed? Sleeping in that same bed with her!

Polly could hardly believe her ears when her father suggested it.

"The bed's plenty big for two," said Doc Sutter. "And she's really not sick anymore. Besides," he added, "I'm sure Paul is getting tired of sleeping all cramped up on that bench."

"Then *I'll* take the bench," said Polly.

And from that night on she did just that—took her pillow and blankets and slept on the fireside bench.

For Polly the next few weeks were almost unbearable. Papa decided that Sunflower should spend some time each day out of bed, so in the morning he would carry the girl out and seat her, wrapped in a blanket, before the fire. In the afternoon, he would carry her back to the bedroom for a nap.

But in the meantime, Polly had to go about all her cabin chores under the dark, watchful eyes of the girl—not able to even grumble about it.

She did not know exactly how much English Sunflower knew when she had arrived, but it was certain she would know a great deal more before she left.

For in the evening Papa would carry Sunflower out again for supper. And then, while Polly was scouring pots, he would sit beside Sunflower on the fireside bench and give her lessons in English. After so many years tending the Tomahawks, Doc Sutter spoke their language as if he were one of them himself.

Polly didn't like it one bit: that her father and this strange Indian girl could talk and smile together without Polly knowing a word of what passed between them.

One evening the lesson might be on clothing, with Sunflower's tongue getting tangled on such words as "jacket" or "leggings." Another night her father might focus on all the cooking utensils that hung on the fireplace hooks. "Kettle" and "ladle" were especially difficult mouthfuls for Sunflower, but she seemed to delight in the word "spoon." She would say it over and over

For some reason Sunflower loved the word spoon.

and laugh each time she said it. One time after she said "spoon," she looked over and smiled at Polly, who sat at the table sewing.

Polly caught herself just in time. *She had almost smiled back!*

What Polly hated the most was when Doc Sutter taught Sunflower how to say the family names. Her Indian tongue made PAH-WUL out of Paul and PAH-LEE out of Polly.

Polly ground her teeth when the girl said PAH-PAH. That was just too much—that her father should teach an Indian girl to call him *Papa!*

During the lessons one evening Polly again sat sewing. She could not help but notice what a truly beautiful girl Sunflower was now that her face had filled out and her hair had been washed. Again Polly struggled with the fact that the girl was older than she. Though Papa had said the pneumonia was all gone, Sunflower still looked small and frail and a good deal paler than most Indian girls.

Yet she certainly seemed to have enough spirit—especially when Papa would begin the lessons.

Why he continued to carry her out of the bedroom, like an invalid, Polly could not understand. After all, if Sunflower were to eventually go back home to her tribe, she ought to start walking now to get back her "sea legs," as the Boston sailors put it.

And why should Papa want to teach her more English? What good would that do her when she was only going back to her tribe?

And why hadn't someone from the tribe come seeking her after all these many weeks? Polly knew Indian girls were in no way considered as important as Indian boys, but she could not believe the Tomahawks would simply allow the Great White Doctor to carry off one of their girls and never bring her back.

Polly's needle stopped in midair.

Suddenly an awful fear took hold of her. Was Papa teaching Sunflower English because she was *not* going back?

Had her father made some kind of a deal with the Tomahawks for Sunflower to stay and live with them? Here in Chappie Creek—*in this very cabin*?

Her Secret Heart

8

Her Secret Heart

DEAR DIARY, Polly carefully wrote as she sat alone before the fireplace. She was always most careful in her writing and she only wrote in the little red leather book when she had something really important to say. She knew that once the book was filled up, there was no guarantee she might get another. In fact, she was probably the only girl in Chappie Creek who had her own private book with blank pages.

The diary had been her mother's—brought from the East—and that was another reason why the book was so precious to Polly. Even if the front pages were missing.

Polly knew it was her father who had torn the pages out and had hidden them away in some special place—the way he probably had the memory of Mama tucked away somewhere in a secret corner of his heart. He never talked about Mama, but Polly often found him sitting before the fire with a sad, faraway look on his face and she knew then he was thinking about Mama.

Polly often wondered what secrets her mother might have shared with the little book. She herself wrote things she would rather die than have anyone else know about.

Only the little red book knew that Polly Sutter wrote her own poems. Sometimes they were three or four lines. Sometimes they were long and dreary. Like the one she wrote last year when it had seemed the long winter would never end.

DUET

Is it not in endless quest,
    that—whistling out the door—
Which moves the curtain to and fro
    and knocks my night lamp o'er;

A howling, lonesome thing, it,
    that scurries up the snow,
Or darts along the pathways,
    in search, now high, then low?

Is it not a sore lament—
    that dismal wail and moan—

A bleak, abysmal grieving
   for the leaves that once were blown;
A hopeless cry for hilltops,
   upholstered in rich green,
A melancholy query
   for the blossoms nowhere seen?

Yet, it does not seek alone
   or mourn in solitude,
For, I, too, have grown weary
   of the winter's barren mood.

I, too, search—yet vainly—
   for the lavish sweep of bloom
That, banished helter-skelter,
   has fled from winter's broom.

So, I sit here glumly,
   by the window—feeling blue,
All medicined and camphorated,
   wrapped up with the flu,

Joining in the mournful dirge,
   while hopeful yet that soon
Spring will come; then wind and I
   may gaily change our tune!

Going farther back in the small book, Polly
found those terribly sad four lines she had written one night, thinking about Mama's lost baby.
Even today she could not read them without
getting a little lump in her throat.

I never held you in my arms,
I never heard you cry,
I still don't even know your name—
Why did God let you die?

And then there was the one she had written one summer's day, out in the woods, sitting on a log. She thought it was quite clever the way she had arranged the words so they resembled a tree:

I
do
not
think
the arms
of trees are
raised in praise
to Him, our God; but
rather that they do submit
as humble servants to
His sod. Would that I might
likewise be: less proud, more
humble
like
a
tree.

What had she been thinking of when she had written *that* one? Perhaps it had been on the day when she had learned the truth about Emilie Coulter and her Indian grandmother.

Perhaps she had been asking God to help her. Even now, Polly would occasionally feel a little sting of sadness, remembering what good friends she and Emilie had once been.

But maybe there were some things even God could not change: the way a person felt deep, down in her own heart. Especially the way she felt, now, about Wilting Sunflower.

> Is there no wind
>   to blow away
> This deep, dark
>   shadow on my day,
> That hides the bright-
>   ness of the sun,
> Or must I simply
>   run—run—run?

No. She laid her quill aside and carefully recapped the small bottle of blue ink. She would not write that. She would not write anything in the little red leather book today. She did not want to pour out her bitterness on those few precious pages.

Besides, tomorrow she was going to church and she wanted to press out the wrinkles in her one and only Sunday dress.

Good News

9

Good News

AS SHE CAME UP THE AISLE of the small Chappie Creek church, several people turned and gave Polly cold, unfriendly glances. They were the folks who had relatives buried up on Massacre Hill.

But as she took her seat, the Reverend Humphries looked down on her from his pulpit and gave her a warm smile. Polly's pastor knew, as did everyone else in town, why she had been away from church and school for so long. He no doubt considered it a great act of charity that Polly Sutter would spend so much time tending a sick Indian girl.

And whether or not he had planned it, the Reverend spoke to his flock that morning on the matter of loving one's neighbor.

Polly did love most of her neighbors. Especially Lorna and Douglas Howlett and their beautiful baby—even if little Laurie *had* been helped into the world by Emilie Coulter's grandmother.

She was especially fond of Ma and Pa Chappie—now in their 70's—who had built the very first cabin along the creek. And the Fairfields, although sometimes she was annoyed by their five mischievous boys.

In fact, Polly could say she "loved" practically everyone in Chappie Creek—all except Otis Grimes, and that was mostly because he frightened her. And the Coulters, all of whom were part Indian, and the Good Lord certainly could understand that.

And, surely, God did not expect Polly Sutter to love *Wilting Sunflower!*

Polly's spirits had been somewhat brighter that morning as she had dressed up in her Sunday best and gone off, for the first time in weeks, to Sunday services.

But now she was once again thinking gloomy thoughts about her father and the Indian girl who took up so much of his time.

So concerned with his Little Sunflower, Doc Sutter seemed to have almost forgotten that Polly even existed. And more and more was Polly convinced that her father did not intend to take Wilting Sunflower back to her tribe.

The bed's plenty big for two, he had said.

Polly shuddered at the thought of getting under the same quilt and sleeping in the same bed with the Indian girl. What was Papa thinking? Surely he must know how hard it had been for Polly these many weeks. Why should he want to make it even *harder?*

The only thing that had kept Polly going was the thought that someday Sunflower would be gone and life would be as it once was in the small cabin: just Papa, Paul, and herself.

Now, Polly felt like some small, trapped animal with nowhere to run.

. . . unless you want to make the trip alone.

Before the Sunday service was over, the Reverend Humphries made two announcements. The first was that Emilie and Mary Elizabeth Coulter needed help on their committee to plan the coming spring social.

Polly Sutter did not, of course, add her name to the committee list. She wouldn't have—even if the Reverend had not made his second announcement: that in less than a week the stagecoach was due to arrive in Chappie Creek.

A Face in the
Window

10

A Face in the Window

SHE WASN'T SURE JUST WHEN she had decided—perhaps it had been 'way back on that day when she lay on her bed, before Wilting Sunflower had arrived.

But now Polly knew what she would trade with Homer Farnsworth for the stagecoach fare east. She hated to part with them, but she knew they were valuable and was sure Homer would not hesitate making a trade.

The old man's shaggy eyebrows went up as Polly laid the mother-of-pearl comb, brush, and mirror on his counter.

"Yours?" he asked cautiously.

"Yes. They were my grandmother's."

He picked up each item and examined it more closely. "And what would you consider a fair trade?"

"Gold," she said simply.

And again the old man's eyebrows went up. For most of Trader Farnsworth's business was just that—trading. When a settlement woman wanted a bolt of fabric she might offer several dozen eggs in exchange. Another family, whose hens might not be laying, would bring in some honey in exchange for a dozen eggs. And so on.

Rarely was there a demand for money—unless something had been ordered and delivered by stage from the East. And then that, of course, had to be paid for in gold. The same as passage on the coach.

"Ah!" said Trader Farnsworth, nodding. "You've some business with that stage due in tomorrow."

"Yes," Polly nodded, praying he did not suspect just what her business was. For the Chappie Creek trading post was also the place where folks traded information—and gossip. If Homer Farnsworth had the slightest notion that Polly Sutter planned to get on that stagecoach, it wouldn't be long before the whole town would know about it. Including her father.

Polly tiptoed into her bedroom to hide the small pouchful of gold in her bureau, under her linen petticoats. She carefully opened the drawer so as not to wake Sunflower who was taking her afternoon nap.

She glanced over her shoulder as the Indian

There, in the window next to the bed, was a face!

girl turned over in her sleep. And then Polly let out a gasp. For there, in the window next to the bed, was a face!

She slammed the drawer shut and ran out of the room. Paul was cleaning his gun and her father was sitting before the fire reading the weeks-old newspaper that had arrived by Pony Express.

"A face!" she gasped, pointing to the bedroom. "In the window!"

"Probably just a bear," said her father, turning a page.

"No! It looked—looked *human!*" But, had it—really?

"Paul, go out and take a look," said her father, calmly.

"Sure, Pa." Paul put on his jacket and, with his rifle under his arm, went out the cabin door. It wasn't long before he was back and rehanging his jacket on its peg. "It was nothin', Pa. Just Crazy Otis, pokin' around outside again."

Doc Sutter looked up. "Otis Grimes?" From the tone of his voice, he seemed not to think that Otis Grimes "poking around" outside the cabin was *nothing*. "You saw him at the window?" he asked Polly.

"Well, I saw *somebody*—"

To Paul: "And this isn't the first time?"

"Been around once or twice before," answered Paul.

"You let me know if he ever comes around here again," said his father firmly.

"Why?" asked Paul. "What harm could one crazy old—"

"A *great deal*," said Doc Sutter. He laid his newspaper down and got up from the bench. When he turned to his two children, his voice was deadly serious. "There's something both of you should know about Otis Grimes."

"Oh, Pa," said Paul, "everybody knows—"

"*Nobody* knows," said Doc Sutter. "Only those Indians, Otis himself—and me. And I didn't know until just this morning when I found him up on Massacre Hill, talking to himself—half out of his head."

Both Polly and Paul slowly came to the hearth and sat down on the bench. What was Papa talking about? Why, there wasn't a person in Chappie Creek who didn't know Otis Grimes was crazy in his head with grief over the death of his wife and baby.

"Everybody knows—" began Polly.

"Everybody *thinks*," he corrected her. "Everybody thinks they know what's been eating away at him these past 15 years—that Otis Grimes is crazy with grief. But, it's not grief—it's *guilt*."

"Guilt!" brother and sister exclaimed at once. What should Otis Grimes feel guilty about?

Their father nodded toward Massacre Hill,

and in her mind Polly could see it all: the Indians whooping and hollering and swooping down from that hill—

"Those Indians," said Doc Sutter, "were out of their heads. Crazy. Because they were blind drunk."

Polly's jaw dropped open.

"They were drunk on white man's brandy. The applejack Otis Grimes made himself and had traded to them just the day before. And that's why Otis Grimes is losing his mind," said Doc Sutter. "He knows that he himself killed his wife and baby."

"Oh, *no*!" said Polly, covering her eyes. "What a terrible thing to have to live with!"

"He *can't* live with it," said her father. "So he keeps telling himself it wasn't his fault—it was the Indians. That's the only way he's kept on going. Keeps telling himself it was the Indians, and every day he's hating the Indians more and more.

"But every now and then he remembers whose fault it *really* was." Doc Sutter looked in the direction of Otis Grimes' rundown farm. "I've seen Otis—how he looks and how he acts—and I know now that someday soon he's going to go over the brink and convince himself one way or the other.

"And then he's going to kill either himself— or an Indian."

Paul again went out with his gun, this time to scare up some fresh meat for their supper. His father went into the bedroom to check up on the napping Sunflower.

Polly put some beans and honey to bake and then sat on the bench, watching the logs crackling on the hearth.

Papa could be wrong. Even a doctor can make mistakes—especially when it comes to somebody else's mind. How could Doc Sutter know what was going on in Otis Grimes' head? Had he opened it up that morning and looked in?

How could he be so sure that Otis Grimes was going to kill anybody?

Still, she wondered if she should tell Papa that it was Otis Grimes who had wanted—and now had—the old tomahawk. She had thought that maybe he was going to use it to bury the hatchet. What if Papa was right and Otis intended to bury that hatchet deep in someone else's skull?

. . . Injun up to yer cabin?

. . . only because she's sick.

Gonna die?

Not if my father can help it.

Maybe your pa won't be able to help it.

Was that someone Wilting Sunflower? Was that why Otis Grimes was poking around outside the cabin—watching and waiting for the right moment?

No, Polly thought. Otis Grimes would not want to kill a sick Indian girl who had nothing to do with the tragedy of Massacre Hill.

This is what Polly wanted to think. And her own mind refused to go back to that day when her father had first laid Wilting Sunflower down on the canopy bed.

I'll kill her, Polly had thought.

And even if Sunflower might be in danger, didn't she have two staunch and loving protectors: PAH-PAH, the Great White Doctor, and PAH-WUL, the Great White Hunter?

Besides, Polly Sutter had more important things on her mind. Tomorrow she was leaving for Boston.

Going East

11

Going East

SLIPPING AWAY was surprisingly easy. Paul was up and out hunting before dawn and Polly's father was out helping a new baby into the world.

Polly didn't even look toward the canopy bed as she tiptoed to the bureau for her pouchful of gold and then stuffed it and her petticoats into the partially packed carpetbag she had hidden under her brother's cot. On top of the petticoats she laid her diary and her mother's cameo brooch. Last of all she placed an old letter that bore the address of her Aunt Clara in Boston.

When she tiptoed back out of the bedroom, she still didn't look toward the bed. If she had, she would have seen that it was empty.

How dark and still the settlement was before dawn. Especially the woods.

Polly had decided to cut through the woods instead of taking the path. It might take her a bit longer to reach the trading post, but there would be less chance of being seen by some early-rising neighbor.

She wondered if she should not have said more in the note she had left on her bureau. But what more was there to say than simply:

Papa, I have gone east.
Polly

Would he even care? For that matter, would he even know who *Polly* was?

She swallowed hard against a sudden bitter lump in her throat. No! She was not going to cry. She was finally going east and it was good-bye, forever, to Chappie Creek with all its hardships and heartache.

As the first glimmer of dawn began to creep into the forest, the still, leafless trees became whitish and ghostly, like silent, disapproving watchers. But, at least now she could see and could make her way through the maze of trees without every now and then bumping into one of them.

She was almost out of the woods when she heard the first terrified scream.

At the second scream, Polly dropped her carpetbag and spun around.

And then she let out her own terrified gasp. For there—pinned against a tree—was Wilting Sunflower. Holding her around the neck with one hand was Otis Grimes. His other hand, raised high, held the old tomahawk.

And then he's going to kill either himself–or an Indian.

"No!" Polly screamed.

Later she would wonder at her own quickness. But, now—like some wild creature of the forest—Polly sprang at Otis Grimes, and the next thing she knew, they were grappling on the ground, scrambling for the fallen tomahawk.

"Run, Sunflower, *run!*" she managed to gasp through the scuffle.

Sunflower tried to run, but stumbled and fell. Even if she had not fallen, she would not have gotten very far. For Polly, still struggling, learned only then that the Indian girl was *crippled!*

Wasted as he was, Otis Grimes was still stronger than Polly. And soon she herself was pinned to the ground with the man's sharp knee in her middle and his bony hand on her neck.

His eyes were wilder than ever as he reached for the tomahawk.

"Thought you could save 'er? You're no better'n *she* is! Fact, you're worse! Nothin' worse'n an Injun lover! I'll take care of *you,* first!"

And he slowly raised the tomahawk.

Dear God, prayed Polly, closing her eyes. *Don't let it hurt too much. Let it be quick!*

It *was* quick. A sharp gunshot pierced the morning air and Otis Grimes flew up and fell onto his back as if he had been struck by lightning.

A small wisp of smoke trailed from the muzzle of his gun as Polly's brother came out of the trees.

"Dead," was all he said as he looked at his sobbing sister, and then at Otis Grimes, lying lifeless on the ground.

A Second Note

12

A Second Note

THEY BURIED OTIS GRIMES up on Massacre
Hill, next to his wife and baby. There was only a
handful of people there—the Reverend Humphries and a few Chappie Creek menfolk to
shovel the dirt back over the dead man's grave.

Doc Sutter was not there, for he was attend-
ing to the living: taking the crippled Sunflower
back to her tribe.

Polly spent the morning sitting home by the
fire, still shivering with shock over the terrible
happening in the woods. She stirred only to
open the door for the Reverend Humphries and
quietly let him into the bedroom where her
brother still lay sobbing.

Poor Paul. He had begun retching as soon as
they had gotten back to the cabin—retching as

if he were determined to throw up his very insides. And then he had begun to sob—deep, moaning sobs that tore at Polly's own insides.

It must be terrible, she thought. To kill a wild animal was one thing. To have killed a man was another.

She drew a deep sigh of relief when the sobbing finally stopped and the sound of two voices came softly through the bedroom door. She knew then that the Reverend Humphries was practicing his own brand of healing: leading her tortured brother in prayer.

It went on a long time, but eventually the voices stopped. And then Paul and his pastor came out of the room.

"Your brother is going to spend a few days down in the valley," said the Reverend. "There's a lot of mending on the old church that needs a pair of strong, young hands."

It was almost twilight before Papa finally arrived home. When he quietly sat down beside Polly on the bench, he seemed drained of all energy—as if the day's events had been too much for him, too. It was some time before he spoke.

"That was a mighty Christian thing you did out there in the woods, Polly."

Still in a daze, Polly looked at her father as if she did not understand.

"Greater love hath no man—than that he lay

down his own life for a friend," quoted her father.

"*Paul* saved her life," said Polly, looking away. "Not me."

Doc Sutter studied his daughter a few moments. "Hurts even to admit it? That you risked your own life for an *Indian?*"

Polly kept her eyes from his. Had she actually done that? And if so—why? Why should she care enough about Wilting Sunflower to want to save her life?

Doc Sutter reached into his shirt pocket and took out two folded slips of paper. He slowly opened them and then laid them in Polly's lap. One she immediately recognized as her own farewell note, left on the bureau. The other had some Indian markings on it—probably scratched out at the fireplace with a piece of charred wood.

"*Both* running away," he said sadly.

So, that was why Sunflower had been in the woods. She, too, had been running away from Chappie Creek!

"I had wanted her to stay," said Doc Sutter. "I had hoped you and she could have become like sisters."

Once again Polly turned from her father.

"But it could never be. I should have known from the start that she would, in time, get the sickness."

"Sickness?" Sunflower had long ago become well. What new sickness did she now have?

"The same sickness your mother had," her father said quietly. He gave out a deep sigh, and then silence hung heavy between them like the newly awakened memory of Polly's mother.

Polly got up and began stirring the soup that was simmering on the hearth.

"Your mother was sick a long time," her father finally said.

"Yes—I know," said Polly.

"No. You *don't* know. Because it was before the dead baby—before even *you* were born."

Polly stopped stirring and stared at her father.

He nodded toward Massacre Hill. "And even before that."

Polly continued to stare, almost fearful of what her father might say next.

"The Indians didn't kill your mother, Polly," he said, getting up from the bench. "*I* did."

Eyes wide, Polly watched her father as he walked to the bedroom door and then stood looking at the canopy bed. He said it slowly and painfully.

"Your mother died of homesickness, Polly."

Polly lay in the canopy bed, unable to sleep. She barely remembered having cooked and served supper, or whether either of them had

"Papa," she said softly, "I have to know."

even spoken at the table. All she could think of was what her father had told her about her mother.

That was why her mother had been found dead at the trading post. She had not merely been wandering, out of her mind, but was waiting for the stagecoach. She was finally—after ten long, torturing years—going back home.

Polly suddenly shivered in the bed. If Polly Sutter herself were to make it to Boston, a part of her mother would also make it back.

I had hoped you and she could have become like sisters.

That was why Doc Sutter had been so attentive and fatherly to Wilting Sunflower. He had hoped that in giving Polly a sister he might lessen her yearning for the East.

Although she had found the answers to many questions, it was what her father had *not* told her that kept Polly awake. The question gnawed at her like hunger pains—the hunger to know the whole truth. Finally she could bear it no longer.

She got up from the bed and went to the bench where her father sat staring at the fire. She knelt on the rug and gently laid her hand on his arm.

"Papa," she said softly, "I have to *know*."

He wearily nodded, as if he had been sitting up, waiting for the question.

"Papa, if you knew Mama hated it so much—that she was so homesick for Boston—why didn't you take her back?"

He studied the fire as if in its warmth and glow lay the answer.

"I couldn't go back east, Polly—not unless I could take *all* of my family."

Confused, Polly sat back on her bare heels. "*All* of your—"

Doc Sutter nodded westward to where the Tomahawks lived. And then he finished softly, "My *other* daughter, Polly—*your sister, Sunflower.*"

The Whole Story

13

The Whole Story

POLLY THOUGHT she was going to faint. Her
father thought so, too, for he suddenly caught
her as she swayed toward the fire.

Then he lifted her up, and with her head down
on his shoulder sat down again on the bench.

"I know, now, Polly that I should have told
you a lot of things a long time ago. This is the
second time I made that mistake."

And then, by the flickering fireside, Doc Sutter told his daughter the whole story.

Young Matthew Sutter had been studying in
Boston to be a doctor. But after a while he grew
weary of the long hours over his books, and
when a group of adventuresome young men decided to go west, Matt Sutter packed up and
went with them.

He had eventually ended up in Chappie Creek where everyone thought he already was a doctor. Including the Indians. It was during his visits to the Tomahawk camp that he grew to know and become fond of the chief's young daughter, Shining Star.

Matt Sutter did not refuse the chief's offer of his daughter in marriage in return for his medicine and healing, and it was not long before the "doctor" and his Indian bride were expecting a child.

But something went wrong and Shining Star died right after the baby was born. Matt Sutter blamed himself for not being a *real* doctor, so he left his baby daughter, Shining Sunflower, in the care of the Tomahawks and went back to Boston to finish his studies. That was when he had met and married Polly's mother.

"I told her my first wife had died," said Doc Sutter. "I *didn't* tell her the girl had been an Indian and there had been a child. Not until we were settled in Chappie Creek and you and Paul were on the way.

"I know it must have been a terrible shock. I myself was shocked to find that Sunflower was crippled." He gave out a deep sigh. "I'll never forget the day I brought the child to the cabin. Your mother became hysterical.

"It was a punishment, she told me, that Sunflower was born crippled. God did not plan that a white man should marry an Indian. She thought God would continue to punish the white doctor, and *all* of his children would be born crippled.

"She believed that—even after you and Paul were born. It was not until each of you took your first steps that she was convinced you both were strong and straight.

"But even that didn't help, and more and more your mother began to think about Boston. So much so, that it began to eat away at her, crippling her mind."

"And Sunflower?" Polly asked, not having said a word throughout her father's sad tale.

"Your mother forbade me ever to bring Sunflower back to the cabin. And she hated it every time I went off to the Indian camp."

Like me, thought Polly.

"I know Sunflower has never really been happy," said Doc Sutter. "Even though she is the chief's granddaughter. You see, Polly, some of the Indians have their own ideas about white men marrying Indian women—and Sunflower has always been somewhat of an outcast. Especially among the women. Being crippled makes it even worse, because she can't do her share of the women's work." He sighed again. "Still, it's the only life she has known—and she finally grew homesick for it."

They were both silent, then, father and

daughter seated on the bench, thoughtfully staring into the fire.

"Does *she* know?" Polly finally asked. "Sunflower—that she's my sister?"

Her father nodded. "She knew for quite some time that I was her father. She didn't know she had a sister—and a brother—until I brought her here."

"Did she know you wanted her to *stay?*"

He nodded again. "But she couldn't. That's what she wrote in the note. She could not live—"

"—with a sister who hated her so much," said Polly painfully.

He nodded wearily. "I didn't tell *you*, Polly, because I wanted you to accept her—maybe even love her—first."

Polly stared at the fire a few moments and then looked toward her room, to the empty canopy bed.

It's plenty big for two . . .

She suddenly burst into tears and buried her face on her father's chest. "I didn't hate her, Papa! I was just—"

"*Jealous?*" he said, drawing her close. "Thought I didn't have room in my heart for *both* of you?"

Doc Sutter gently stroked his daughter's hair. "Polly, I love *all* of my children."

Going West

14

Going West

ONE BRIGHT SPRING DAY Doc Sutter saddled up two mares he had borrowed from one of their neighbors.

"What's this?" said Paul, coming out of the cabin. "*Both* going off and leaving me alone?"

"Afraid so," said Doc Sutter. He gave Polly a wink as she got up onto one of the mares. "After all, no doctor worth his weight in quinine ever travels without his own nurse." With a flick of the reins he slowly led his own horse and the extra mare out of the yard.

Polly followed. She didn't even look toward Massacre Hill. Or if she did, she really didn't see it.

All Polly could see were the small spirals of smoke to the west that meant the Tomahawk camp, the home of her sister, Wilting Sunflower.

But not for long, thought Polly. Before sundown, there would be three returning to Chappie Creek.

117

The Wonderful World of Children's Books

" Reading about a character is a lot different than seeing him on TV. You can get to know him better—get more deeply involved with him as a person—in a book, because you're with him a lot longer. **"**

Barbara Reeves, consultant
to "Sesame Street"

IN GRANDMA'S ATTIC. Ever explore an attic? It's lots of fun—especially when the strange items one finds cause grandma to tell neat stories about the olden days. Fifty years ago, in a big farm house in Michigan, a girl used to explore her grandma's attic . . . and ask questions about the strange things she found. The stories her grandma told are in this book: how a beaded basket led to a scary adventure with a hungry Indian . . . the time grandma took a dare, and nearly froze her tongue on the new pump . . . why grandpa was so positive the shoes a neighbor offered him would fit, because "when the Lord sends me shoes, he sends the right size."
77271—$1.25

Handy order form
on last page

The Wonderful World of Pop-Up Books

Favorite Bible stories that "Pop Up" . . . full-color scenes, often three dimensional . . . figures lift from the scene when page is turned . . . other figures move when tabs are pulled.

The Shepherds' Surprise. Child opens book, and shepherds raise up from the page . . . child pulls tab, and angel appears in the clouds.   82362—$3.95

The Life of Moses. Hebrew slaves push a big stone, chariot moves, bush burns, waters part . . . all as child turns pages, pulls tabs, etc.   82370—$3.95

Jesus Lives! Gethsemane scene appears in 3D as book opens . . . Jesus appears in upper room when tab is pulled . . . He ascends into clouds as page turns.
82388—$3.95

Noah's Animal Boat. Amazing action—Noah's saw moves and sounds . . . animals and ark appear in 3-D . . . ark tosses on the waves. More, too!   82396—$3.95

Handy order form
on last page

The Wonderful World of Teen Paperbacks

Fire! You'll find mystery in this tale of Ann and Rob, who spend a summer with their aunt and forest-ranger uncle. They look forward to adventure, but they find more than they really want. Can the two teenagers help discover who is starting the forest fires? More important, can they help lead their unbelieving uncle to a greater discovery?   82974—$1.25

Tanya and the Border Guard. Tanya lives in Russia, where visible Christians are often persecuted. When her family and friends worship, they must gather secretly in a forest. Was Tanya wise to reveal their meeting place to the soldier, even though he did say he was a believer? She'll soon find out—because now he and two more soldiers appear at their little meeting in the forest!   75994—$1.25

Alexi's Secret Mission. For Christian activities, Alexi's family is banished to Siberia. Alexi has to give up his friends; worse yet, he can't be on the school team because he's a Christian. He almost resents his faith! But soon he's involved in something more exciting than sports—spreading God's Word. And what does that service to God bring him? Read fast!   87338—$1.25

Turkey Red. When Martha's farming family came to America for religious freedom, they brought a special variety of wheat—red wheat. It grew well in Kansas, but no one would buy red wheat. Brother Jake had other troubles: prairie fires, rattlesnakes, Indians; so he ran away to the city. And for Martha . . . a real problem of the time: should she mix with children who didn't belong to their church? Important lessons in sharing!   89482—$1.25

Handy order form on last page

The Wonderful World of Teen Paperbacks

Never Miss A Sunset. Put yourself in Ellen's place:
75 years ago, on a backwoods farm in Wisconsin.
Ellen is 13. She loves her family, but resents being
second mother to her nine brothers and sisters. Then
tragedy brings Ellen a guilt heavier than all her chores
—a terrible burden that remains until winter warms
into spring . . . to bring a time of new understanding
for Ellen and her mother.   86512—$1.95

City Kid Farmer. Won first prize in David C. Cook's
1975 children's book contest! You'll sympathize with
Mark; he has to give up his friends when his folks
move to the country. But worse, his aunt and uncle are
just as "religious" as his mother. You'll see how Mark
adjusts to rural life . . . and the chain of events that
leads him to know Christ himself.   89474—$1.25

Pounding Hooves. More than an exciting horse story—
it's the story of Lori's jealous struggle with her friend
Darlene. Darlene probably will win the art contest.
She'll win Ken, too—Darlene's so pretty! And Storm,
the beautiful Arabian stallion—Darlene's father surely
will buy him before Lori saves enough money. Rivals
for so much . . . even with God's help, can Lori
overcome her jealousy of Darlene?   89458—$1.75

Captured! Teenage adventure in wilderness America!
Captured by Indians, Crist and Zack strike a bargain.
The Indians want to learn more about the white man's
ways, so the boys agree to teach the Indians—if they
will spare their lives. But the boys would rather return
home. Why, then, does Crist pass up a chance to
escape? And Zack—why does he escape . . . then act
so strangely when he finds the chief's son wounded,
and helpless?   87312—$1.50

Handy order form on last page

The Wonderful World of Picture Strip Books

The Adventures of Tullus, teenage Christian in ancient Rome. Tullus fights for his faith against the terrors of his time. Exciting adventures in black-and-white picture strips, with fast-moving dialogue! Each book 112 pages.

Tullus and the Ransom Gold. Can Tullus find enough money to free his Christian friends from death in the arena? He does —but then finds himself in the arena . . . defending a girl from a savage lion. What can he do!   77057—$1.25

Tullus and the Vandals of the North. Go with Tullus as he explores the outer limits of the ancient Roman empire . . . see how faith and prayer help him turn trials into opportunities to win others for Christ.   81249—$1.25

Tullus and the Kidnapped Prince. Would you risk your life for a savage young prince in faraway India? Tullus does. See why!   84152—$1.25

Tullus in the Deadly Whirlpool. Can Tullus convince the sailors he's not to blame for the storm and whirlpool that threaten their ship? He must convince them. But how?   77065—$1.25

Boxed gift set of 4 books. $4.95

Christian Family Classics. Two famous stories—"Ben Hur," and "Christian Family Courageous." Learn how a youth in Bible times overcame tremendous adversity. Read how a shipwrecked family provided for its needs on a tropic island. Both stories told in black-and-white picture strips, dialogue, captions.   81786—$1.25

Handy order form on last page

The Wonderful World of The Picture Bible

Easiest way imaginable to read the Bible—all the drama and excitement unfold vividly in black-and-white picture strips, easy-to-read dialogue, and captions.

All illustrations and statements authenticated by Bible scholars for biblical and cultured accuracy. Enjoy reading these 6 volumes:

OLD TESTAMENT

Creation: From "In the beginning" to the flight from Egypt

The Promised Land: Moses, Ten Commandments, Jericho

The Captivity: Divided kingdom falls . . . Israel is taken into captivity . . . prophecies of a coming Messiah

NEW TESTAMENT

Jesus: The Life of our Lord—His birth, ministry, first followers, crucifixion, and triumph over death

The Church: Angels announce Jesus will return . . . Pentecost . . . Stephen is stoned . . . Paul's conversion, missionary ministry, and death . . . the end of an era.

82701—All 6 books in slipcase. Set, $6.95

Handy order form on last page

The Wonderful World of Magic Picture Books

Bible stories—plus! Each book tells a favorite Bible story in words children 4-8 understand and love. Every page has a full-color illustration, and also a "magic" blank spot that's a source of surprise and delight when rubbed with a pencil.

BIBLE STORIES

Set 1: One! Two! and You ● Here's My Donkey ● Strange New Star ● Jonah ● God Made It Good ● Ruth's New Home   70920—$1.95

Set 2: What Shepherds Saw ● Up the Sycamore Tree ● Ring, Robe and Shoes ● Colorful Coat ● David, the Giant Killer ● In a Lions' Den   70938—$1.95

Set 3: Down Through the Roof ● Lost Lamb ● Night Ride to Egypt ● Jericho ● Gideon's Warriors ● Baby Moses   70946—$1.95

Set 4: The Birth of Jesus ● Jesus Lives! ● Noah's Ark ● Queen Esther ● Why Seas Grew Calm ● Shadrach, Meshach, and Abednego   70953—$1.95

LIFE RELATED STORIES

Set 101: Ranger Treemore's Flowers ● Rabbit That Changed Colors ● Frisky's Christmas Tree ● Ants! ● Bear of a Different Color ● A Special Treat.
86934—$1.95

Set 102: Too Many Blackberries ● Lolly and the Christmas Cactus ● Frisky Pup Playing Possum ● Katy's Kittens ● No Eggs for Barney ● Why the Fish Grew
86942—$1.95

When a child rubs a pencil over one of the blank spots, a story-related activity appears. It may be a drawing, words, dot-to-dot puzzle, crossword puzzle, etc.

Handy order form on last page

The Wonderful World of Children's Books

THE SHAWL OF WAITING

Maybe you'd have done the same, if your grandmother had told you such a strange story. Anyway, after hearing her grandma's story, Emilie Coulter started to knit her own "shawl of waiting." Emilie knit, and knit—even if she didn't believe her grandma's story. But the more Emilie knit, the smaller the shawl became! Why couldn't she finish it?   89466—$1.25